# Searching for
# CHRISTMAS

## Holly Ann Gardner
### Illustrated by Wes Wheeler

CFI
AN IMPRINT OF CEDAR FORT, INC.
SPRINGVILLE, UTAH

ISBN 13: 978-1-4621-2278-3

Published by CFI, an imprint of Cedar Fort, Inc.
2373 W. 700 S., Springville, UT 84663
Distributed by Cedar Fort, Inc. , www.cedarfort.com

Library of Congress Control Number:  2018946722

Cover and interior layout design by Wes Wheeler
Cover design © 2018 Cedar Fort, Inc.
Edited by Kaitlin Barwick and Nicole Terry

Printed in the United States of America

10 9 8 7 6 5 4 3 2 1

# Add a musical touch to story time with inspiring original songs by composer Blake Gillette!

When you see the music note symbol 🎵, pause your reading and listen to the track that is listed at the end of the text on that page. Once the instrumentals start near the end of the song, begin reading the story again where you left off.

## List of Tracks

1. Do You Believe?

2. Searching for the Savior

3. The World Is Yours

4. Children of Light

5. Denali's Song

At the top of the world, where it is cold and white, where it is quiet and frozen, where all you would expect is snow and ice, is a place called the North Pole.

There you will find a tiny crimson cardinal named Denali.

Denali is a Christmas Cardinal, and she has been entrusted with a very important job.

Her job is to sing! She practices all year so that on Christmas morning she can chirp her beautiful Christmas melody for all in the North Pole to hear.

One year, as Christmas was drawing near, Denali should have been flitting around with excitement, but she found herself struggling to find the spirit of Christmas. She knew that there was only one person who could help her . . . Santa!

So Denali set out to see Santa and to find her Christmas spirit.

As Denali flew, she noticed others busy about. She saw a tall evergreen being decorated. She noticed a mother hare with her bundle of fluffy white babies hopping through the snow. She saw a handsome snowman being built. Oh, Denali did love snowmen! But Denali did not falter, for she had to be on her way.

At last Denali reached her destination: Santa's cottage! She earnestly tapped on the wooden door. The sound of Christmas cheer escaped through the cottage and settled in her petite ears. The sugary-sweet smell of Christmas found its way to her eager nose. Finally, Denali found herself being greeted by Santa.

She also found herself shy, unsure, and embarrassed. She lowered her head and managed to say, "I need help finding my Christmas spirit."

A floating hush suspended in the room until Santa knelt down and scooped Denali up in his mild hands. He looked at her gently and spoke to her soft and clear.

"I love Christmas! I delight in being Santa Claus, and I adore the festivities of the season! Christmas truly is magical. But, Denali, do you know what I love the very most?"

"I love my Savior Jesus Christ!" Santa exclaimed. "It is He who I worship. It is He who fills my heart with joy. He is why I celebrate! So, my tender, precious Denali, in your pursuit to find your Christmas spirit, search for your Savior. Look for Him, for He is all around you.

"He was born a tiny babe in a humble stable. He came to save the world. He came for me and He came for you. Celebrate His birth, His life, His love. Clear your eyes, open your heart, and let His spirit fill your soul." ♫

Denali sat still for a quiet moment. She brushed away an escaped tear from her cheek, and with timid determination, she sailed away with a new longing and a bright hope.

♫ 1. "Do You Believe?"

Denali turned to deliver a silent "thank you" to Old Saint Nick. As she directed her gratitude toward the cottage, she was amused at the sight.

She blinked away the cloudy fog and looked upon the house with new eyes. Her gaze fell on the intricate wreath that adorned the gate. She followed the pattern in a perfect circle and noticed that it was unbreakable and everlasting.

The flicker of the candle's flame in the frosted window caught her attention. She pondered on how just a fragment of light could cut through the darkness, bringing security and comfort.

Beyond the glow, she was granted a glimpse of Santa; even he appeared somehow different to her. Her dearest Santa, so merry and gleeful. *Perhaps*, she concluded, *because he is so selfless, so giving, and so generous.*

Understanding flowed through Denali. Faith whispered to her. "Search for your Savior" lightly echoed from within. A tingling in her heart told her that she had indeed felt Him there.

Traveling toward her nest, Denali inspected the handiwork of the now-grand snowman that stood so proudly in the meadow. A smile turned up her cheeks, for the snowman got the better of her, and she simply couldn't resist his charm.

A bundle of peppered white fluff curled quietly atop the snow suddenly blinked.

"Why excuse me," said a startled Denali. "I did not mean to wake you."

"Not at all," replied the kind old fox. "That's my job, you know. I've been making snowmen longer than I can remember, but he isn't quite complete." Defeat lingered in the eyes of the poor, tired fox, and a sympathetic offer to help rolled out of Denali's tiny beak.

"I know just the thing!" And away she flew.

At first sight of her return, the worn fox experienced a jolt of excitement, his puffy tail swirling about uncontrollably. He watched as Denali placed a sprig of holly on the brim of the snowman's top hat and then hung a peppermint candy cane on the twisted branch that was the snowman's arm.

With a beat of her hushed wings, she settled alongside her new friend. "Oh, thank you, thank you—he is indeed a noble gentleman after all," said the fox. Denali listened to the fox tell tall tales of the "good 'ole days" and of times forgotten. She heard countless adventures of shaping snowmen of grandeur that the once-frisky fox presented as his annual Christmas gift for all to enjoy.

The meek fox turned to her and asked, "Do you think my gift this year will be accepted?" Silence cascaded down with the now falling snow.

Reaching out and tenderly touching the fox with her feathered wing, Denali answered, "You have given all that you have to give, and you have done your very best. You can now rest, my kind, weary friend. Your gift is a gift of love. There is none greater than that."

The words "Search for the Savior" repeated in her thoughts.

A rush of warmth rolled over her as she adored the enchanted expression of love and gratitude from her unexpected friend, the humble fox. 🎵

Denali paused briefly to enjoy the quickening in her breast and the fervor expanding in her heart. Once again, He had found her.

🎵 2. "Searching for the Savior"

Denali barely felt the sting of the bitter early night breeze as she happened to flutter past the mother hare. "My baby—he has vanished!" cried out the hysterical mother. Seeing the worry in the eyes of the distressed hare, Denali calmly offered her assistance.

Flight and a keen eye played to her advantage as she maneuvered her way through the frozen forest in pursuit of the lost youngster. Discouragement was taking hold as Denali looked for a tiny parcel of ivory fur among the fallen snowflakes.

Persistence bestowed a kind favor that cold evening as Denali caught a glimpse of the little runaway. Speaking softly, she told the frightened baby that if he would follow her, she would lead him safely home.

He bounded voluntarily after Denali, excited to be reunited with his family. A hopping jubilee shook the ground as he was encircled by twitching noses and long ears.

Denali helped corral the cluster of bunnies down into their cozy underground den. She took upon herself the challenging chore of putting the babies to bed. Defeated in her attempt, she experimented with an old lullaby. She filled the cavern with a tender tune that enchanted the little ones into a peaceful slumber. ♫

Several tiny stockings hung with anticipation of losing their emptiness. The smell of cinnamon and spice danced among the ribbons and the bows. Denali saw a glorious porcelain angel, so perfect and pure. A glimmering golden halo suspended above her intense blue eyes and her pearly pink lips. Oh, how Denali yearned for her to speak, fantasizing of her angelic message.

"Search for your Savior" called to Denali once again. Noting that the worn-out mother had finally fallen asleep, Denali whispered a "Merry Christmas" and a soft "Sweet dreams." As she briefly stayed in this home so full of love, she was firmly aware of His presence and knew that He visited here often.

♫ 3. "The World Is Yours"

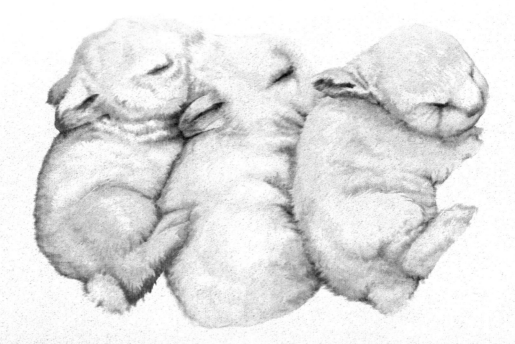

Music and laughter spiraled heavenward with the winter wind as Denali continued toward her nest. Curiosity caught Denali in the current of merriment and guided her to the giant evergreen.

Glee sparkled in her eyes when the celebration came into view. Creatures big and small sang yuletide carols as they took on the task of decorating the massive tree. ♫

Denali clasped an ornament in her beak, but a reverent awe entrapped her as she peered up at the breathtaking sight. Twinkling lights burned like a billion stars, blinking the tree to life. Tinsel encircled the tree from bottom to top in a loving embrace. Intricate ornaments of silver and gold hung in proud silence as they reflected the lights' glow. The majestic tree, so splendid and regal, pointed to the heavens, giving praise to its maker as the blazing star radiated its light for all to see.

♫ 4. "Children of Light"

Denali approached and added her meager effort by adorning the tree with one more ornament.

"Search for your Savior, Denali" resonated from within. There at the foot of the tree, there among her closest friends, there in the eve of Christmas, Denali closed her eyes and let Him in.

Resting her wings under the sweeping blanket of the darkened sky, Denali recalled the events of the day.

She had started out hollow, glum, and longing. That was before—before Santa's sacred lesson, before the wreath and the flickering candle, before the holly and her newfound friend, before the rescue, the lullaby, and the angel, before the lights, the ornaments, and the love of friends. That was before Denali knew how to search, before she took the time for understanding.

Denali found the example of unselfish giving, she found sacrifice and wisdom, she found unwavering love and patience, she found companionship, but most of all, she had discovered the source of eternal light. She had regained her Christmas spirit; it was secure inside her, burning and warm. For in her search she had indeed found her Savior.

As the rays of the resurrected sun emerged from their slumber, Denali awoke, perched high on her branch. Christmas had arrived! With all the love that Denali possessed, she began her song.

She sang not only for the North Pole but also for the world. She welcomed in the blessed day of the Lord Jesus Christ's birth. A trill of hosanna danced upon the radiant sunbeams as they caressed the wintry horizon. ♫

Denali trembled as her love flowed from within her. She cried to the heavens her sonnet of gratitude. Denali was a Christmas Cardinal. She would forever share her Christmas melody to those who would listen, and she would evermore echo the words, "Search for the Savior!"

♫ 5. "Denali's Song"